WEST SLOPE COMMUNITY LIBRARY
16

COOPERATIVE
ES

D0130890

THE FLIM-FLAM FAIRIES

by Alan Katz

Illustrated by Michael Slack

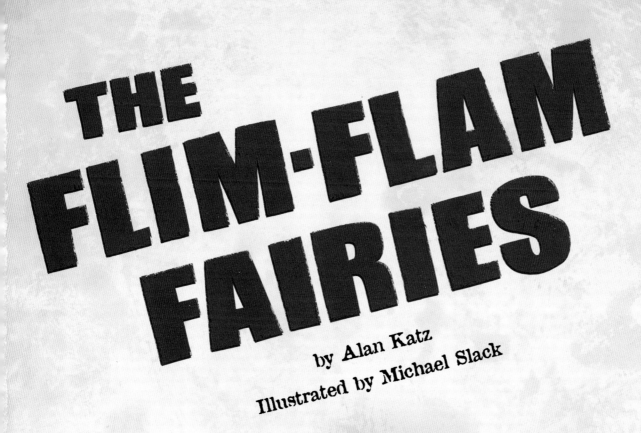

WEST SLOPE LIBRARY
3678 SW 78th Ave.
Portland, OR 97225
(503) 292-6416

RUNNING PRESS
KIDS
PHILADELPHIA·LONDON

TO DAVID AND NATHAN,

two boys who are more magical than
any fairies could possibly be.

—AK

TO PHYLLIS A SLACK,

my personal tooth fairy. Thank you for your love and
support, and encouraging me to pursue my dreams.

—MS

Text © 2008 by Alan Katz
Illustrations © 2008 by Michael Slack

All rights reserved under the Pan-American and
International Copyright Conventions

Printed in China

*This book may not be reproduced in whole or in part, in any
form or by any means, electronic or mechanical, including
photocopying, recording, or by any information storage and
retrieval system now known or hereafter invented, without
written permission from the publisher.*

9 8 7 6 5 4 3 2 1
Digit on the right indicates the number of this printing

Library of Congress Control Number: 2007920260

ISBN 978-0-7624-2996-7

Cover and interior design by Frances J. Soo Ping Chow
Edited by T.L. Bonaddio

This book may be ordered by mail from the publisher.
Please include $2.50 for postage and handling.
But try your bookstore first!

Published by Running Press Kids, and imprint of
Running Press Book Publishers
2300 Chestnut Street
Philadelphia, PA 19103-4371

Visit us on the web!
www.runningpress.com

For hundreds of years, kids have been
LOSING TEETH
and putting them under
THEIR PILLOWS.

Each time, the Tooth Fairy comes, takes the tooth, and leaves a small gift—like a quarter or a book.

How sweet. How kind.

HOW LOVING.

How Sickening!

Allow me to introduce myself.

I AM THE BELLY BUTTON LINT FAIRY,

and I've got a new and exciting deal for you!

WAIT'LL YA HEAR THIS!

Just pick the lint
out of your belly button.

MAKE SURE TO GET IT ALL.

And put it under your pillow
(but don't try to mix in
any lint from the clothes dryer!).
You'll have swell dreams, and while
you sleep, I'll . . .

WAIT!
WAIT!
WAAAIT!

THAT'S **NONSENSE!**

DON'T touch your **BELLY BUTTON LINT,**

and **DON'T LISTEN TO HIM!**

Listen to **ME** instead! I'm the **Earwax Fairy!**

GRADE **A** WAX

It's EASY, FRIENDS!

Just put a gob of earwax
under your pillow, and in the morning
you'll awake to . . .

Now you might be asking,
why does the Earwax Fairy want my earwax?

What will he do with it?

And do you know what I say?

WOW, YOU ASK A LOT OF QUESTIONS!

So just take the earwax and put it . . .

HOLD IT RIGHT THERE!

Kids, **NEVER, NEVER, NEVER** put your fingers—or anything else—in your ears! It's not healthy. And there's absolutely no reason to place earwax or belly button lint under your pillow!

Because there's only one thing

that truly belongs there . . .

DIRTY UNDERWEAR!

Dirty underwear is a marvelous thing, and when you put it under your pillow and go to sleep, I will come take it and you will amazingly wake up 14.6% smarter than when you went to bed. I know it sounds too good to be true, but it's the 100% cotton-pickin' truth!

EVERYTHING THOSE GUYS HAVE BEEN TELLING YOU IS WRONG!

Don't you dare

put **DIRTY UNDERWEAR** or **EARWAX** or **BELLY BUTTON LINT**

under your pillow!

EVER!

Who am I?
I'm the

CLIPPED TOENAIL

Fairy!

Millions of foolish folks
throw out their clipped toenails every day.

They don't realize that if they'd just put them under their pillows,
I'd swoop down in the middle of the night, collect those
delightful trinkets, and in their place leave a shiny new . . .

Here's an important news flash from your pal **THE SNOT FAIRY**: lose the lint, whack the wax, undo the undies, and ta-ta to the toenails! Keep those things right where they belong—**IN** you, **ON** you, or whatever! And here's what I want you to do instead:

I pay $1.12 each. And sometimes I throw in a bonus of $3.46 for the

SUPER-STRETCHY KIND.

So rememb . . .

NO PICKING! NO PLUCKING! NO YANKING!
NO TWEAKING! NO SCOOPING!

And keep your dirty underwear to

YOURSELF!

I'M . . . pizzzzzert . . .

THE FART FAIRY!

Kids, just make sure to pass some gas under your pillow, and I'll reward you with an enchanting treat!

MY PLAN IS TO RUN THE WORLD ON NATURAL GAS— GET IT, NATURAL GAS?

I'll bet you didn't know that

ONE SINGLE FART

can keep a street lamp lit for over 17 minutes! And that can go up to 19 minutes if there are beans involved. So, to save the environm . . .

Now just hold your **FART-FILLED HORSES!** Kids, do not listen to that **NONSENSE!** In fact, do not listen to **ANY OF THEM!**

But please listen to **ME**, because I've got an idea I'd like to throw up to you! Understand what I mean? **THROW UP TO YOU?**

Yes, that's right, I am the one and only Pu . . .

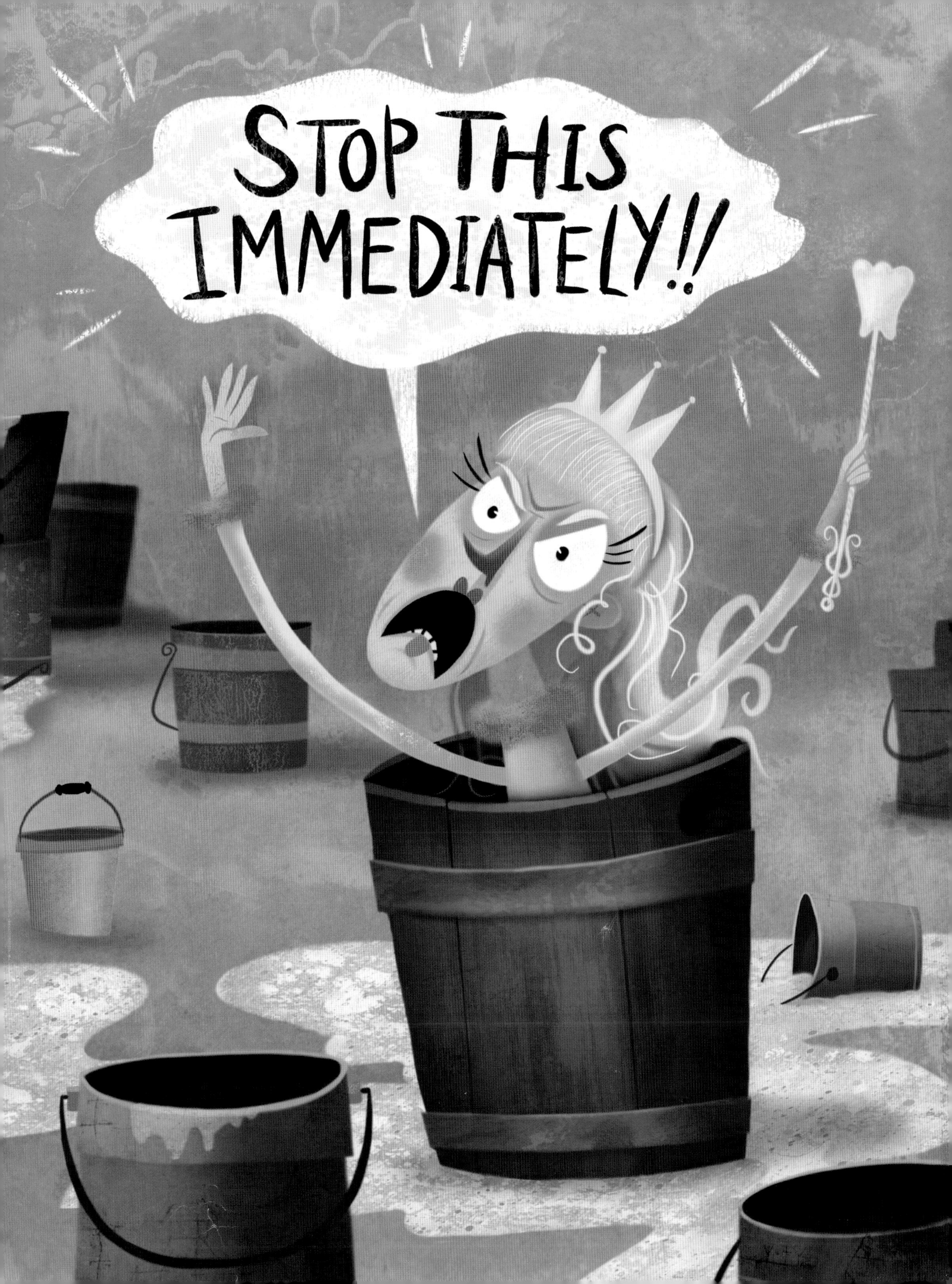
STOP THIS IMMEDIATELY!!

GREETINGS!

I am the Tooth Fairy.

The honest to goodness Tooth Fairy!

This book has been

a ridiculous parade of fake fairies

and flim-flamming fools!

DO NOT BELIEVE
ANY OF THEM.
DO NOT DO A SINGLE THING
THEY'VE SUGGESTED!

Remember, when you lose

a tooth, place it under your pillow,

go to sleep, and you will likely

find something

SPECIAL

when you awake.

BUT IF I SEE belly button lint

or earwax or dirty underwear or

clipped toenails . . .

if I smell farts or any other

disgusting substance

under that pillow . . .

THE DEAL IS OFF!

Oh my,
I got a little excited there. SORRY. Have a nice day.
And be good to your teeth.

TA-TA!

EXCUSE ME...

9/08
E
KAT